You Are NOT a Cat!

Sharon G. Flake · illustrated by Anna Raff

BOYDS MILLS PRESS

AN IMPRINT OF HIGHLIGHTS

Honesdale, Pennsylvania

Boyds Mills Press
An Imprint of Highlights
815 Church Street
Honesdale, Pennsylvania 18431

Printed in China
ISBN: 978-1-59078-980-3
Library of Congress Control Number: 2015958445

First edition
Design by Sara Gillingham Studio
Production by Sue Cole
The text of this book is set in Corn Dog and Kiddy Sans.
The illustrations in this book were made with
sumi ink washes, and pen and pencil drawings
that were assembled and colored digitally.

10 9 8 7 6 5 4 3 2 1

To my niece Munira and my nephews
Makki and Mason, who were born
worthy of every good thing. And to
my sister Veronica D. Flake (Miss Fab)
whose vision and bravery will
forever impact our family. —SGF

For Caleb and Will. —ASR

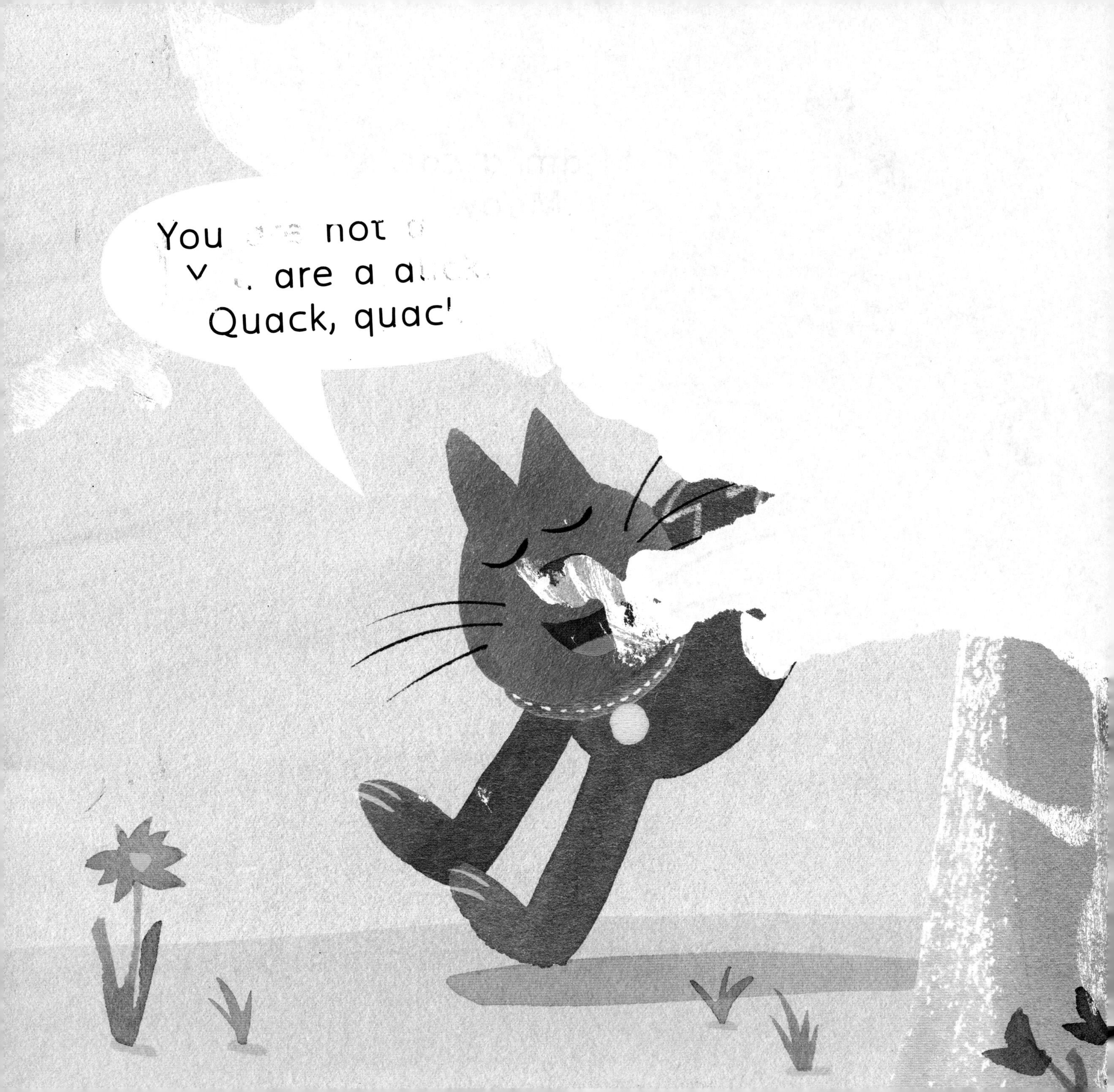
You not
are a
Quack, quac

Meow is what I like to say.

Meow.

Why can't a duck do that?

Because ducks go quack, quack!

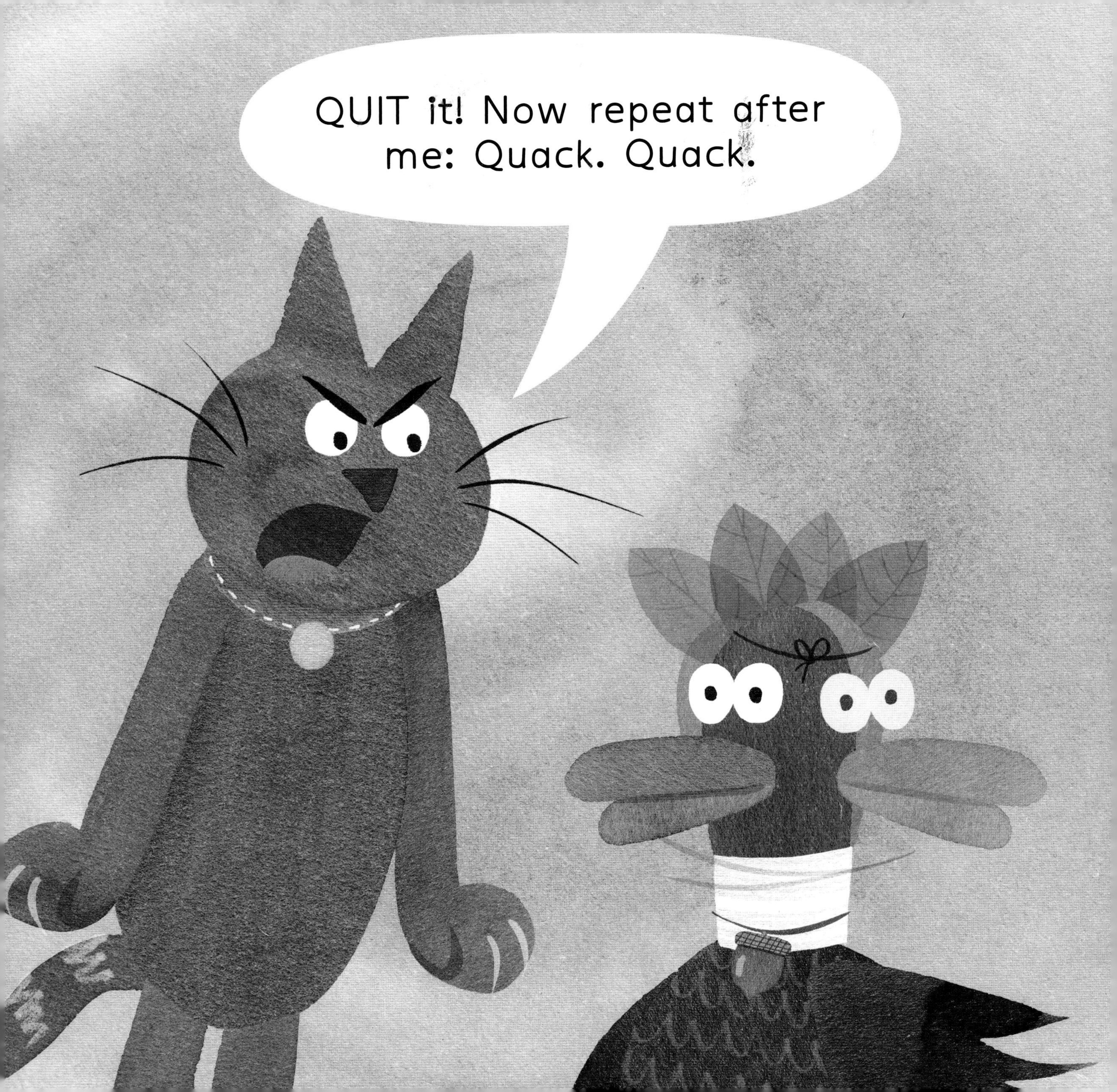
QUIT it! Now repeat after me: Quack. Quack.

Whiskers that tickle the air?

Sharp claws? A taste for mice? A family to love you in a warm, cozy home?

Oh . . . no.

See?
You are a duck.
Look!

Meow.

Nooooooo!

You make nice music
when you quack like that.

Now you're a parrot, I suppose?
I like parrots. They repeat things.

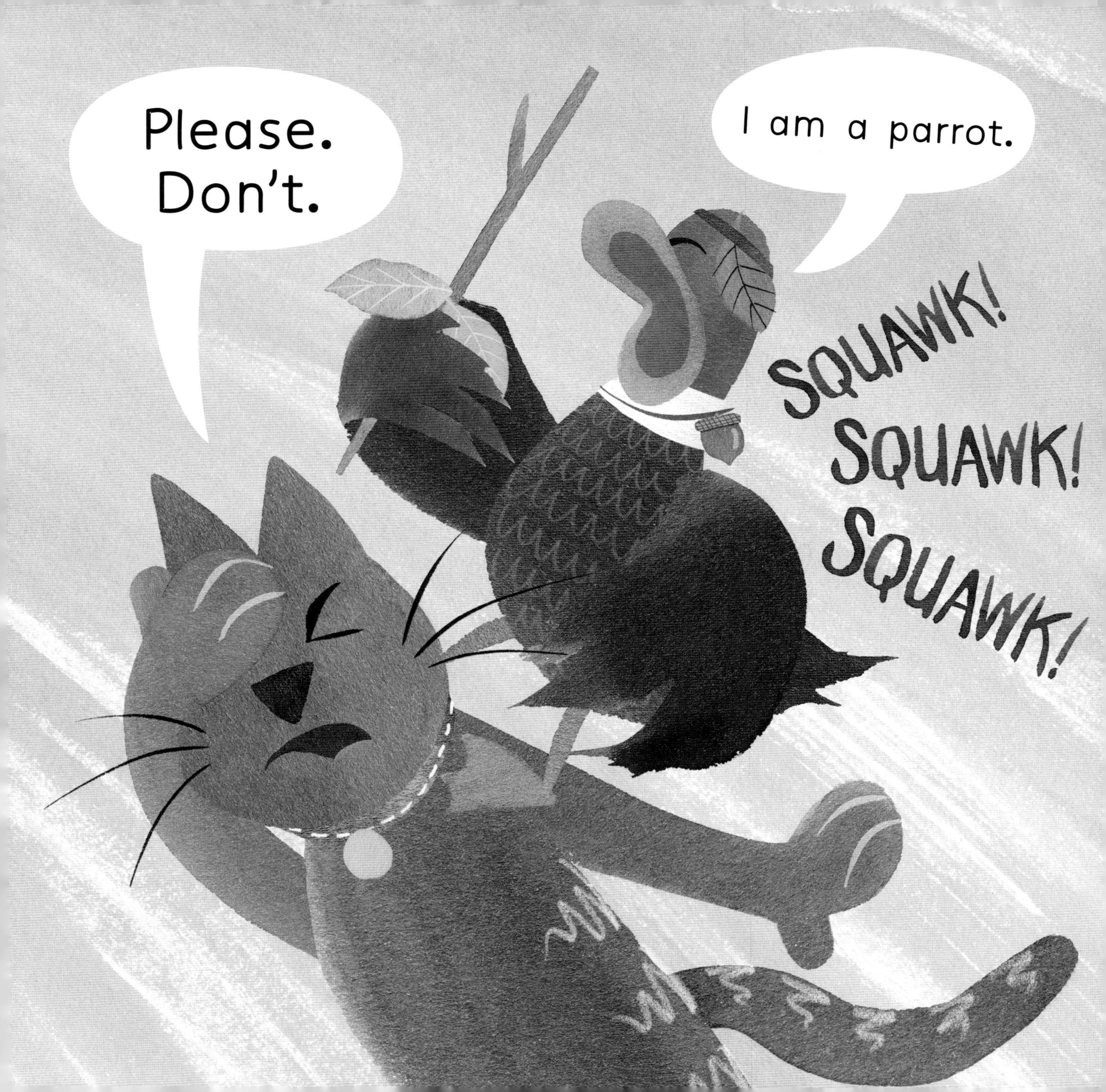
Please. Don't.
I am a parrot.
SQUAWK!
SQUAWK!
SQUAWK!

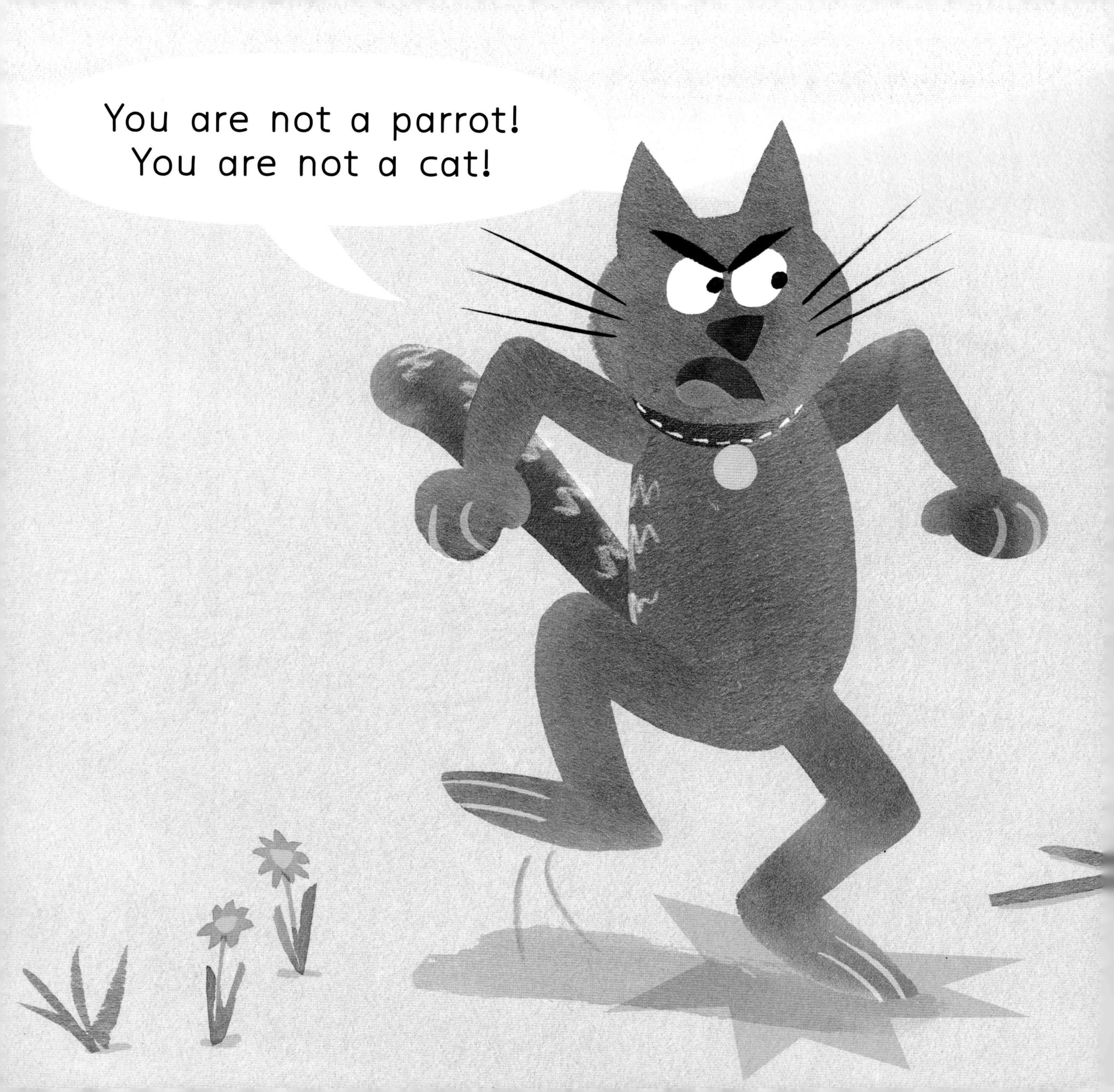
You are not a parrot!
You are not a cat!

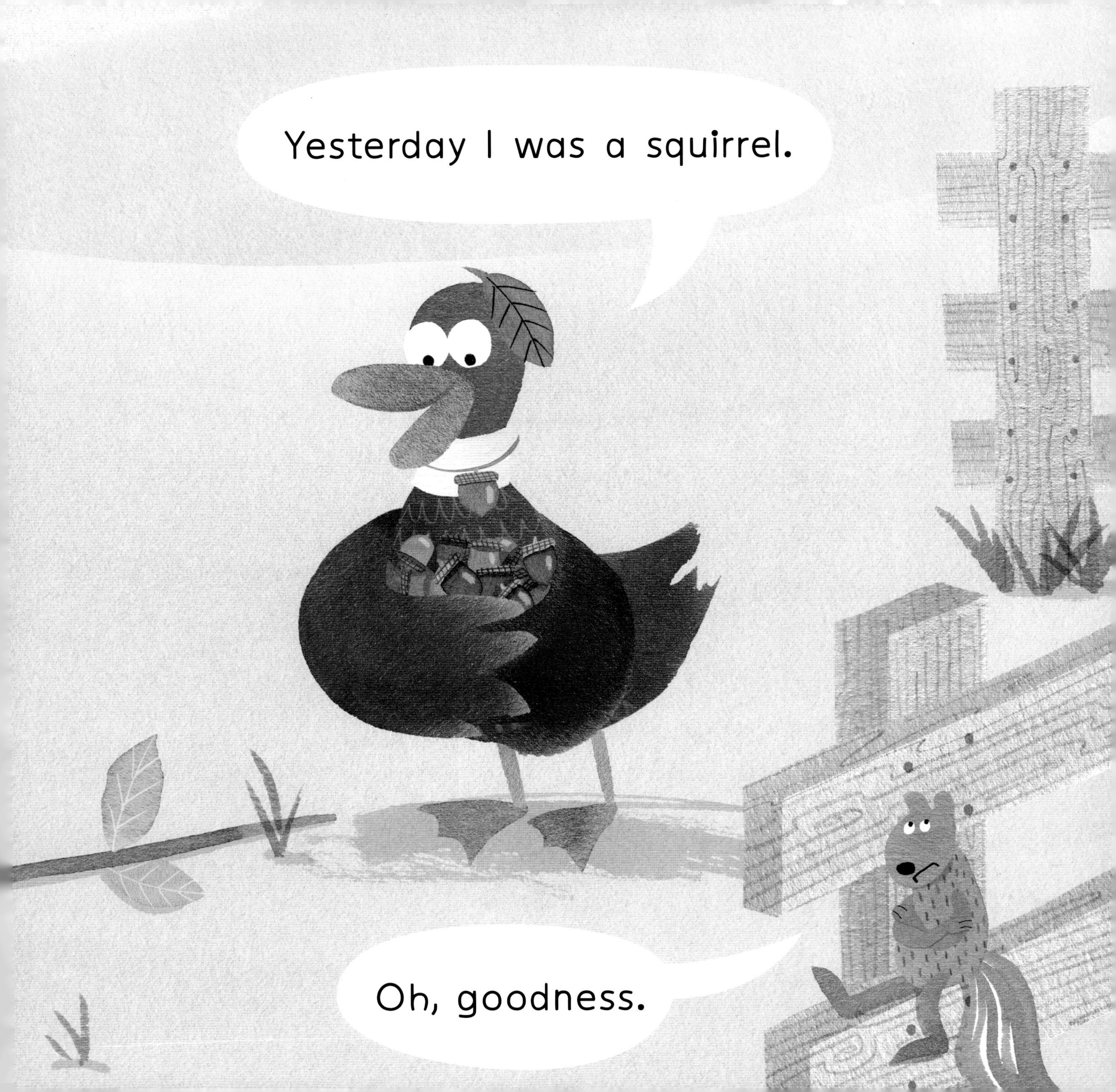
Yesterday I was a squirrel.
Oh, goodness.

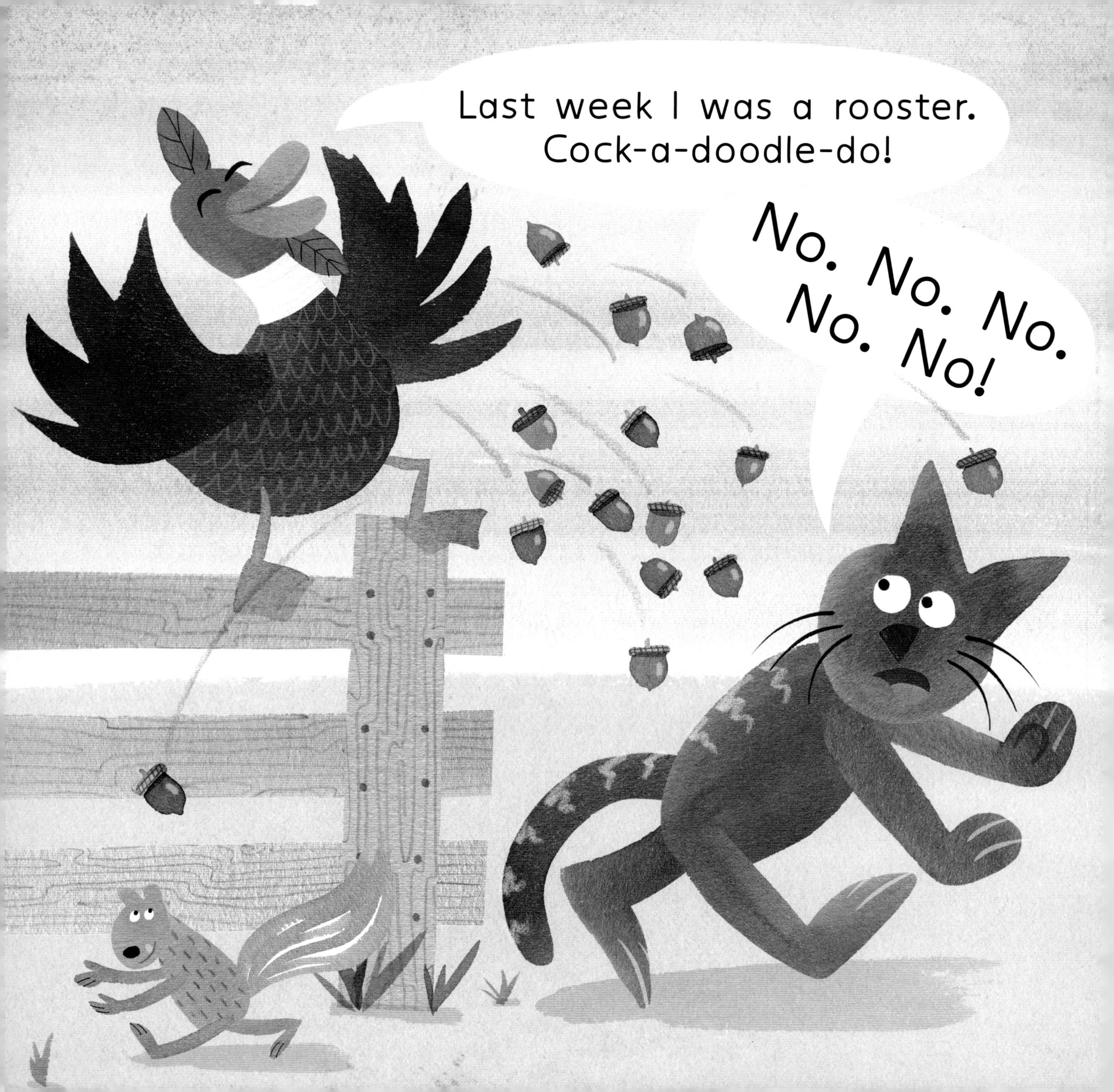
Last week I was a rooster. Cock-a-doodle-do!
No. No. No. No. No!

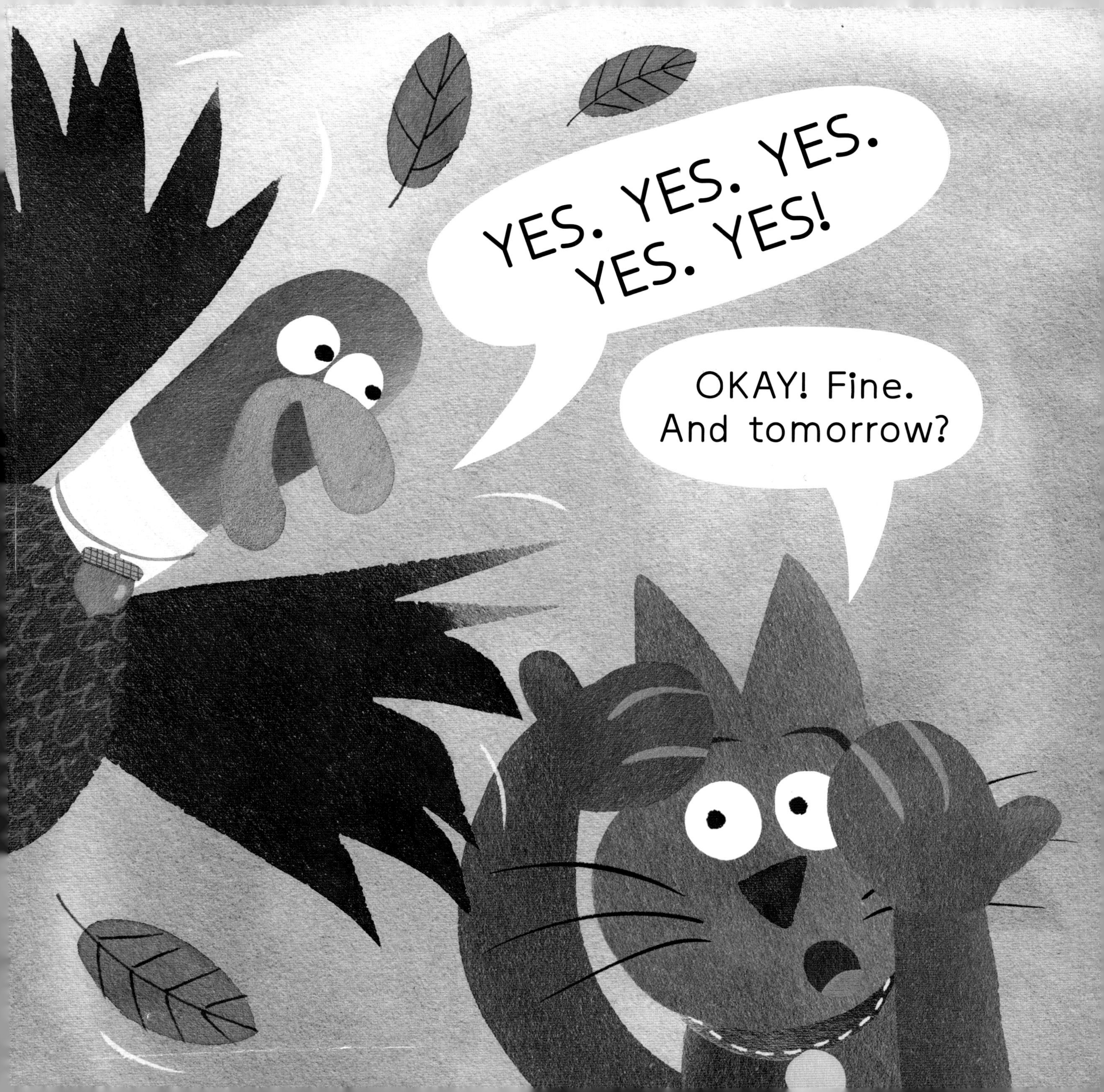
YES. YES. YES.
YES. YES!
OKAY! Fine.
And tomorrow?

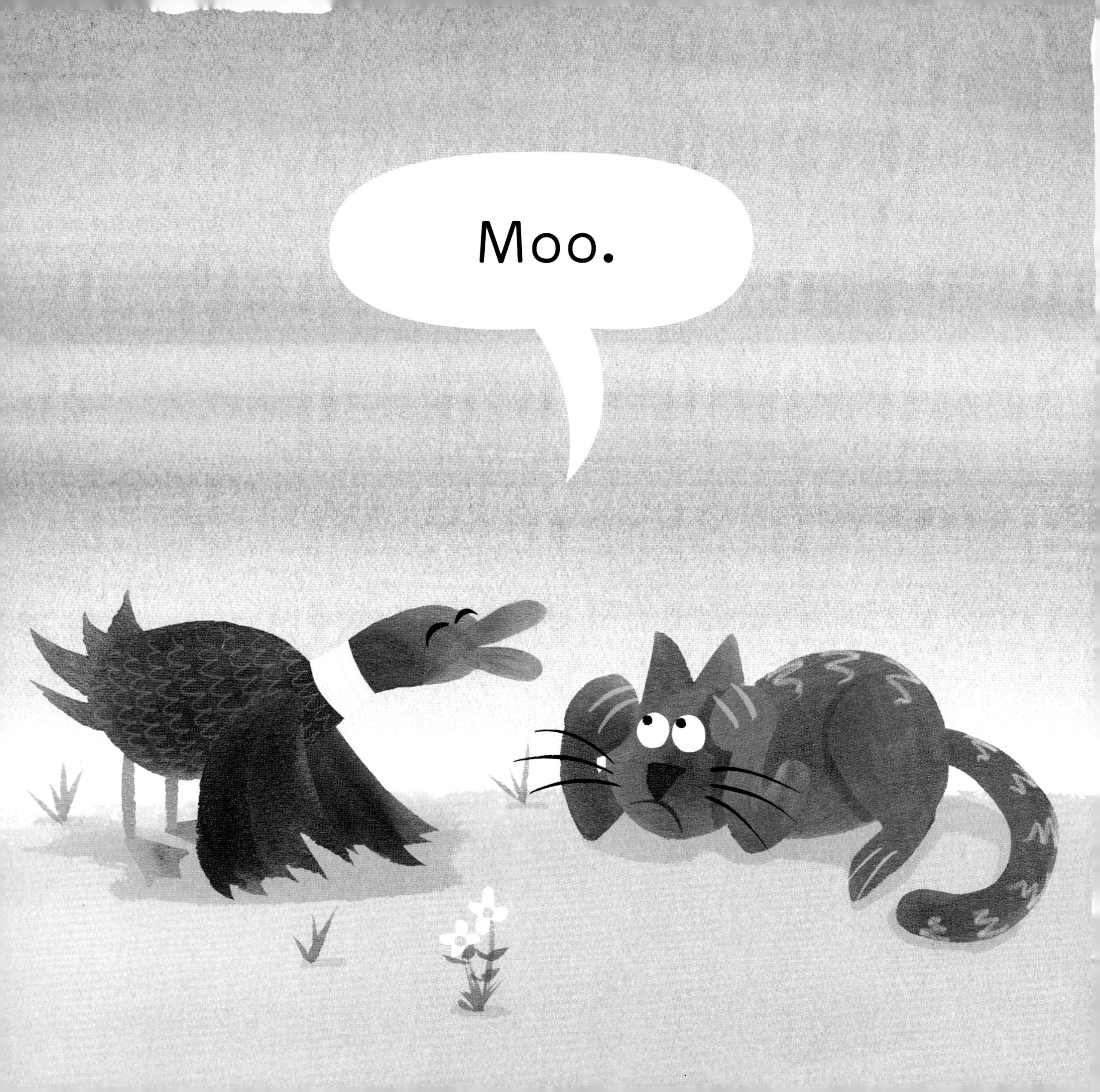
Moo.